Toning the Sweep

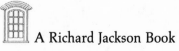

A Richard Jackson Book

ANGELA JOHNSON

Toning
the
Sweep

ORCHARD BOOKS   New York

Orchard Books, 95 Madison Avenue, New York, NY 10016

Manufactured in the United States of America
Book design by Mina Greenstein
The text of this book is set in 12 point Aldus.

10 9 8 7 6 5 4

Library of Congress Cataloging-in-Publication Data
Johnson, Angela.
Toning the Sweep / Angela Johnson.
    p.   cm.   "A Richard Jackson book"—P.
Summary: On a visit to her grandmother Ola, who is dying
of cancer in her house in the desert, fourteen-year-old
Emmie hears many stories about the past and her family
history and comes to a better understanding of relatives
both dead and living.
ISBN 0-531-05476-4.   ISBN 0-531-08626-7 (lib. bdg.)
[1. Grandmothers—Fiction. 2. Family life—Fiction. 3.
Deserts—Fiction. 4. Cancer—Fiction. 5. Afro-Americans—
Fiction.]   I. Title.   PZ7.J629To 1993   [Fic]—dc20
92-34062

To my father,
Arthur Johnson, Jr.,
who told me about toning

Toning the Sweep

❦❦❦ CHAPTER 1

My grandmama Ola says that yellow is the first color she ever remembers seeing. It was just there, she says. Her mama dressed her in yellow, and back in Alabama there were yellow curtains in the kitchen. Their house sat between two willows. They were yellow in spring.

When Ola found out from the doctor that she was sick and wouldn't get better, she says all she thought about was how she'd miss the color yellow. She went home and cooked a pot of corn on the cob and sliced up three lemons to eat.

I write a letter to Ola after I find out she's sick and will have to come live with us.

Dear Ola,

I got sent home early today because I wouldn't stand up and say the Pledge of Allegiance. I really don't know what pledging allegiance is and I surely don't know what doing it to a flag is all about. Anyway, the flag wasn't even there. I think it was sent away to be cleaned. We all looked so stupid standing there with our hands on our hearts, looking at the clock. I couldn't do it.

Mama didn't say much. Daddy just asked me when I thought the flag would come back from the cleaners.

I thought of you when he said that. I started thinking about how much fun we'll have when you get here. I'm sorry you're sick.

What can I send you, Ola, to make you feel better? If there's anything I can do . . .

Peace and Love,
Emily

Ola wrote me back.

Emily,
Come to the desert and smell the flowers.

Ola

꘎꘎꘎ **CHAPTER 2**

In 1964 Mama and Grandmama
Ola left Alabama right after my grandfather's funeral. Ola said that was what Granddaddy would have
wanted. She packed all their clothes up the day he
died—but only the clothes. She left the house and
furniture for anybody who might want it.

My granddaddy'd made Mama a carved wood sign
that spelled out her name: DIANE WERREN. He
made it out of some wood that he'd found lying
around in the shed in back of their house. Mama had
painted it green and nailed it to her bedroom door.
On that hot summer morning it lay in the back of
their new Buick, a convertible with a white interior.

Mama says that in 1964 she sang Supremes songs
so much, Grandmama threatened to take her radio.
Mama hid in the backseat and listened to everything
she could. New cars and the Supremes always make
her think of 1964. She says it was the best year and

the worst year and isn't it too bad that times that still make her laugh and cry are all mixed up in things like singing to Supremes songs and missing her daddy. Uh-huh.

Mama says that she always had big feet—used to stick out like boats from her legs, she says. Even when you'd think she'd have other things to worry about, she couldn't help thinking about her size tens.

That summer the Southwest saw those feet from the backseat of their Buick. She hung them out the window from Alabama to California—so she didn't have to look at them all the time. Didn't change the way she felt about herself, the way her feet were too big and the fact that her daddy was gone. Dead and gone, with them running from the state of Alabama.

Alabama got too big for Mama in 1964—everything happening in that state got too big. You can't get away from the things that make you sad, Mama says. I believe that. Sad can be bigger than happy sometimes.

Mama's been telling me about 1964 on the plane from Cleveland to the desert. I wonder why she's decided to talk to me about all of that now. I can think of about a thousand things to talk about on a plane. Not dead people, though.

But I get a feeling she's telling it all for a reason. Her leaving Alabama when she was fourteen, her big feet, the sign that Granddaddy made for her.

I think maybe I look just like she did in 1964 and it bothers her a lot. I catch Mama looking at me over her newspaper or when I'm just doing dumb things around the house. It seems like sometimes she's almost ready to reach out and touch me like you'd touch your own reflection in the mirror if you came on it real fast. A surprise—a fourteen-year-old surprise to Mama.

All the talk about leaving Alabama and Grand-daddy's dying ends, and I listen to the rumble of the plane. I can see Mama and Grandmama driving over the Mississippi and stopping at the fruit stands on the side of the road when they got hungry.

I wonder if Mama looks just like Grandmama did then, with long fingers and legs.

Every time somebody tells Mama that she has nice long legs, she tells them that she has nice long feet to match them. I say it now too. My legs seem like they go all the way up to my neck—way up my neck, it seems to me.

Mama asks if I am tired and puts on her earphones. It's really like her not to wait for an answer. I don't even think about answering. That's okay too, 'cause I'm just looking out the window and thinking about how long you have to live with somebody to get to know them.

I didn't know that Mama believed in God until I heard her in the bathroom in the airport praying. Just praying like she did it all the time—talking to God like he was her friend Caroline and they were having lunch downtown.

She acted like she knew God, had spoken to him before and everything.

I haven't ever prayed to God in my whole life, 'cause Grandmama told me a long time ago that God was dead. Dead and gone like Granddaddy, goodwill to men, and the passenger pigeons. I knew that she was telling the truth, 'cause she told it to me on one of our walks to the desert, which she calls the dry.

ᵗᵖᵗᵖᵗᵖ **CHAPTER 3**

I've always thought there should
be bones in the desert. Turned white by the sun and
lying on the side of the road for everybody to see so
that they can turn back before it's too late, too late to
get to where it's cool and green. I can't say I've seen
any bones lying on the road outside of Little Rock,
California, though.

Grandmama Ola picked us up at the airport, blast-
ing Supremes music. The Buick, old now, was shin-
ing in the airport parking lot. I noticed it first, then
Ola. She's grown dreadlocks. When she wrapped her
arms around me and Mama, I could almost smell
the desert. Then Ola flew that car into Los Angeles
traffic.

I know it won't be long before the air gets drier
and hotter. Nobody says much, so I just look at the
houses sitting on the edges of hills. Mama frowns a
little when she turns back to look at me. I guess

the traffic noises and Ola driving the old convertible at about one hundred miles an hour sort of bother her.

The green starts to disappear, and I can feel the sun baking my head when Mama turns around again and yells to me, "Girl, you'd better put that hat on your head right now."

I don't think she really wanted to come to the desert. I can barely hear her up front, talking to Ola, who laughs or looks real serious after Mama has said something to her. I figure that Mama kind of feels stuck. She's never liked the desert that much.

I don't feel stuck, though. I hang my head out the side of the car, and my face feels scorched. My throat dries out real quick and the feeling comes back to me that I love the desert. It feels good. All the green is gone now. All the water and the green. I remember any green on the desert almost hurts your eyes, it's so strong.

I tried to explain to Rodney back home how I felt about being in the desert. He didn't get it. Couldn't understand why anyone would like what he called a dead place, with dead plants and crazy people. Rodney said that your brain gets baked by the sun before you know it. I've known Rodney forever, so I just ignored him.

Mama turns around and says again, "Girl, you'd better think about putting that hat on your head. We talked about this before we even got off the plane. I think maybe you're going deaf."

"Not deaf, just brain-fried." I say it low 'cause I think it's what Mama would call a smart-ass remark. It feels good to say it and not get in trouble, though.

Grandmama laughs. She's heard me. Her head is thrown back, and the green scarf that she's tied around her straw hat to keep it on blows across my face. It smells like her.

"It's good to have you here, baby. I missed you and every day I think about you."

I scream over the sounds of the highway that I think about her all the time too, but I don't believe she really hears me. We are in the desert now, and everything feels like it might be brittle or melt when you touch it. I want to tell Ola about how it all feels to me, but I'd have to scream again and Ola's pretty busy passing about a thousand cars and trucks, so I don't say anything.

Ola hits the gas. Mama claims she drives like an Indy 500 racer, but they don't have long flowing scarves that blow in the wind.

My first memory of Ola is of a woman standing by a yellow house wearing a big straw hat tied down with a scarf—yellow and orange blowing in the wind. She looked like one of those women who might garden all the time and talk about rain. She looked like she knew all the proper names for plants. I remember she'd give you iced tea and cuttings from any of her plants and talk about water.

I don't think Ola remembered the Alabama rain she had left in 1964. Ola talked about rain as if it was something that happened on another planet, something that some gardeners got way, way up north. Rain was not something she'd wake up to and hear pounding on her bedroom window.

The one time Ola came to Ohio, she saw the kids on my street open a fire hydrant to cool off and almost had a stroke right there on the front stoop. She kept saying, "The desert is another world." Looked like she wanted to run out in the street and scoop up the small puddles to take back with her to the dry.

Mama's fallen asleep in the front seat, and I look up to see that Ola is half smiling at me. "Where you at, sister? I thought I might have lost you back there. I swear I do believe that you are acquiring my habit of stepping off this world and heading someplace else while conversation is going on all around you."

"I never notice that I daydream so much until somebody tells me a thing over and over."

"Baby, most conversation is boring anyway."

"I don't see you enough to be bored talking to you, Ola. You never ask me about school or say how much I've grown when you do see me."

Ola waves to a group of people who are standing by the side of the road. They call her by name, and she throws her head back and laughs again. I think if I'm lucky one day I'll be able to throw my head back and laugh at what people do or say that easy.

Ola asks now, "How's school, Emily?" I practice laughing with my head thrown back. Then she mimics anybody who's ever told me, "My, how you've grown." Ola's voice sounds like chimes swinging in the wind. She starts to sing whatever the radio is blaring.

I can't wait to get to her house. I can almost see it. Baked yellow. We'll start packing everything, and it'll be like she was never there. It'll be like I was never there too, I guess.

I hope Ola slows down a little.

I've always wondered what it would be like to have a grandmother who sends you cookies in the mail and goes to church on Sundays like most of my friends' grandmothers. One friend's grandmother even knits her sweaters for her birthday.

I can't imagine Ola knitting me anything. She does send me pamphlets on world hunger and the environment. And she sent me a T-shirt from Jamaica when she went there to a reggae festival. Ola has sent me beads from Africa and incense from India, even a case of olives from Greece 'cause she remembered that I hadn't tried them. "You have to try everything if you want to live in this world" is what she always says.

Ola's taken me traveling some. Is that grandmotherly? I wonder. On one of my visits to her, when I was five, we went to the mountains. We hitchhiked with Ola's friend Martha Jackson to get there. I still remember some of the things I saw. I can smell coffee now and still remember all the truck stops and even riding in the back of a pickup truck with hunting dogs. I don't remember the mountains, but I do remember the trip getting to them.

I ask Ola if she remembers our trip to the mountains. She looks real serious, then laughs. "Sure do. There was still snow in the mountains when we went that summer. I carried you on my back, and Martha got bit by some kind of spider that swelled her leg up for a few days. We stayed on that old man's porch overnight until it went down."

I say, "I don't remember that. I remember the dogs in the truck, though."

Mama wakes up yawning in the front seat. She's wearing a shirt that says BE A HUMAN BEAN.

"Have you started packing yet, Ola?" We pull into the driveway. "Everything looks the same."

Mama gets out and walks around the house and looks across at the desert. I only see her back, but I hear her say, "Yeah, everything is just the same."

Ola says, "No, Diane. It's all different. I used to look out and see the desert and think of Alabama and what I could get this place to grow for me. I used to think about how Emily was going to enjoy her vacation here. You know, she looks so much like you I think sometimes I'm twenty-five years younger, hardly grown up myself."

Mama walks into the kitchen and sits down with her knees up to her chin. She is barefoot too. She doesn't go barefoot in Cleveland so much that you'd notice it. We sit in the kitchen, and a hot breeze starts to blow through. I go out on the porch, and it's so white I can almost see the desert bones.

⸜⸜⸜ CHAPTER 4

People used to take pictures of babies that died. I've seen them, pictures of dead babies in their little caskets. Ola used to have some, of her dead cousins. From a long time ago, though. Ola said she inherited them. Like pieces of jewelry or something. The pictures are gone now. She made them disappear. I found them a couple of years ago and started crying when I figured out what they were. Ola called this my sensitive period, when I was about twelve.

Ola's been talking about how she's going to miss everybody out here in the desert. Been thinking about videotaping everybody she'll miss. The idea scares me a little. It's like she's thinking she'll never come back. I think of the babies in caskets.

Mama turns and looks at Ola. Her hands on her hips, she's in fighting stance. She opens her mouth to say something, but stops. She picks up more napkins and looks out the kitchen window. She cusses the heat under her breath and mumbles something like the place is already getting on her nerves. She looks at Ola when she says it, though.

Ola faces Mama. "I do what I want, Diane."

"Yeah, Mama. You've always done what you wanted. It's not like I could say something to you that would change your mind about anything. Anyway, it's too hot to fight with you. Go on—tire yourself out with foolishness. . . ."

Most fights they've had come back to me. There are so many of them. Mama ends up in tears with doors slammed. Ola shrugs and goes about her business like nothing has happened. Since this doesn't look like a big fight, Mama stays in the kitchen, now packing boxes.

Ola stands over the sink, cutting up apples. I keep counting linen napkins for her. She wants to know how many she has. She's going to give most of them away and says she doesn't want to be shamed by any worn ones.

Mama smiles, for a second, 'cause that's what Ola always says. Mama starts marking boxes to go to Goodwill. I put napkins in that won't shame my grandmama.

Ola starts telling a funny story about going shopping with her friend Martha Jackson, and Mama almost falls to the floor laughing, forgetting to be mad. It's good to hear Mama laughing. She hasn't been doing too much of it since we got off the plane.

When Mama stops laughing, Ola says, "I suppose we could get Martha's video camera. Some of her foster kids got her one for her birthday last year, and she's been terrorizing the valley with it ever since. First she made a documentary on some people who were living in the mountains. It almost won some kind of award."

I find a spot of sun on the floor and rest my feet in it. "Martha Jackson sent me a copy in Cleveland," I say. "I didn't really understand what it was about, but the people were strange. Strange and sort of fun. I liked their music and the way they were all so close to one another. Were they gypsies?" I call to Ola, who has gone to sit on the porch.

"No, I think they were just free."

"With the tape she sent me, she wrote a long letter about how she hadn't found people who loved life so much as the people who lived on that mountain. She wrote something about one of the older ones who had the same spirit as her three-year-old great-grandson and she wondered how that could be."

Ola calls out, "Martha's always wondering about something, and I can tell you she's never boring company."

I like Martha Jackson. I can't remember when I didn't know her. You get used to people, I guess.

She's always sending me videos in the mail. I got one of nothing but people's feet. She set the camera up outside a grocery store and just filmed feet for hours. Daddy sat up and watched it with me. We started to make up stories about the people who owned those feet.

Mama came in for a few minutes and watched with us. She said Martha was going through the change, then left the room.

Ola leans against the railing on the back porch. "Mart's been a friend to me for so long I'm already missing her." Ola stares into space and starts laughing.

Mama drags a box across the floor and says that I should call Martha Jackson to tell her we're in town.

"You haven't seen David yet, have you, Emmie?" Mama asks.

"He wrote me in April that he was going to some kind of powwow in Arizona." I was hoping I could go with him. David Two Starr learns all he can about his people. He's lived with Martha most of his sixteen years and is the most serious boy I know.

Once he told me a story about an aunt of his who died young. David's father was three, and his sister was a teenager. Whatever illness she had gave her a high fever, but nobody would give her water. David's father sat in her room hour after hour listening to her beg for it. After a while he went to the pump outside and filled his mouth with water. He made it back to her room without anyone seeing him, then emptied the water into her mouth. He did that until she stopped asking, then sat in a chair and watched the desert get hotter.

I start to think about the people I know in the desert. Mama says people she knew when she first came were considered crazy for living out here. She never really belonged. She says that Ola was running away from things that you shouldn't run away from and ended up here.

I think about how everybody Ola knows here has a story. Daddy says that everybody has one and their stories are all a part of us. If Ola loves these people, then they must be a part of me too. It must be true about all of us being a part of one another like Daddy says.

Ola hums on the porch while Mama eats an apple and labels boxes. I go over to the phone by the refrigerator and call Martha. When she picks up, her voice rings out and is so familiar. I tell her Ola's idea about making a movie.

ಆಿ ಆಿ ಆಿ CHAPTER 5

Martha Jackson's hair is the color of coal and she must be about my grandmama's age. She cuts her hair short, and sometimes it sticks straight up, but she doesn't care.

She's probably one of the tallest people I know, and walks like she's swimming, and that's all the time. She doesn't have a car. Every car she gets lasts about a month. One of her foster kids always ends up wrecking it. It's not something she worries about, though.

Martha looks at you for a long time before she decides to speak. She says it's a habit she got into 'cause her father used to have a bad temper. You had to think before you spoke to him, she says. I'm used to her looking real hard at me.

She's leaning on a Joshua tree in Ola's front yard, saying, "It's like poetry and eating to me now. You let the camera become part of you. Like your head and your eyes. If the camera were to fall out of your

18

hands, it should be like your head falling off in the middle of a conversation."

"I don't know if the camera can ever be that special to me, Martha," I say. "I just got used to the Instamatic my dad gave me four years ago. I can remember to take off the lens cap sometimes."

Martha smiles. "This is a thing to get used to—that's all. No magic, no special real training. Turn the camera on and shoot."

"Guess I'll get it when I chill a little."

I take the camera and start taping a crow that's landed on the back porch. I figure it's a start. The crow gets real interested in me filming him and stops pecking at the old apple core he's found near the garbage cans. He hops off the porch and checks me and the camera out till he sees something else off over by some brush.

Martha's watching me with a smirk when I turn back to her with the camera. "I guess you'll do okay by yourself now." She looks at me for a long time, then says, "Let's talk about Ola."

I start shooting and say to myself, "A part of me," and hope that the thing is going and the lens cap hasn't been on the whole time I've been taping the crow. I zoom in on Martha leaning against the Joshua tree. She stares into the camera.

"I met Ola in the late summer of 1964 'cause there was no other way around it."

A pot falls in the kitchen, and we can hear Ola laughing—then she stops. I keep the camera running.

"Like I was saying," Martha starts to whisper, but changes her mind and speaks even louder, "I couldn't help but meet her. There's about five hundred people that live out here, and she happens to be my closest neighbor. She was playing her music loud one night, and I was sitting out in my yard 'cause there were about twenty kids in my house getting on my nerves."

Ola comes out the screen door and sits down by Martha Jackson. Two people couldn't be more different in looks. I have them both in the frame.

Ola's short and delicate—like she'd break if you held her arm too tight. She wouldn't break, though. She hands Martha a glass of iced tea and sits cross-legged on the ground.

I press the pause button, then change my mind.

Unlike my mama, Ola never wears shoes. She says that her soles can't breathe in them. I decided that my soles couldn't breathe either, even in school. There was some mess with that, and in the end I did just what I wanted to do. I guess most of my teachers decided to ignore me; a couple wanted to torture me but got tired of thinking of things to say. I want to be where I can always be barefoot, so I pan to Ola's feet to remember them.

Ola's saying, "Mart, you would have met me even if I wasn't your closest neighbor because I'm the only one around here who wasn't afraid of you and all those kids." Martha smiles and nods her head.

I sit down on a lawn chair and ask, "What did you two think of each other when you first met?" It's easier to ask what I'd usually think of as a nosy question from behind a camera.

Martha whispers, "I thought she had the worst accent of anybody that I'd ever heard. Never met anybody from Alabama before. It grew on me, though, and I got used to it. I liked her Buick and the way the fool painted the house yellow the day after she and Diane moved in."

Ola spills a little iced tea and says, "No, you didn't. You yelled from the road that this shade of yellow didn't look good from where you stood, and what was it called?" Ola looks at the camera and tells me, "Your mama was so embarrassed, Emmie, she begged me to stop painting it yellow and just make it gray or something. Your mama always took things so much to heart."

"What did you say to Martha then?"

"I told her I didn't know who she was, but if she had enough energy to yell from the road at a perfect stranger, she probably had enough strength to pick up a brush."

Martha tilts her head back and laughs. "So I did."

Ola gets up and goes into the house without making a sound. I don't think that Martha even knows she's gone, 'cause her eyes are closed. . . . She must be meditating. I keep running the camera on her. I get out of the chair and walk backward away from Martha, still taping her as I go.

When I can't see her anymore, I turn the camera off and stand against the side of Ola's house in the shade. It's quiet but not really cool in the shade. Everything is . . . like I've been pushed out of my bed into a bright room. It's so hot in the desert, most of the time I feel like I'm walking in my sleep.

I decide to tape Ola's front yard. It's what she calls a swept yard. No grass, just sand. In the mornings she takes a broom and makes designs in the sand after she sweeps away dead rosebush leaves and brush. I circle the wavy designs and make footprints in the sand. There are three Joshua trees in the front yard, standing around like they're waiting for a bus. I tape them too. It's illegal to chop them down, and I'm glad.

When I was little, I'd have picnics under them. Ola has a picture of me sitting under one tree with no clothes on. I'd run out of the tub to hide. When she found me, I was wearing a lot of sand and a smile. The photo sits on her coffee table, and I love looking at it. Ola calls it a picture of her "sand spirit" child.

I guess thinking about all of this has made me come to what I'm going to tell Ola and Martha. I want to make this movie on my own. Haven't really done that much by myself before, but I feel like I should find out everything about Ola on my own.

Martha comes around the house and looks like she's just got up from a nap. She looks real relaxed and stares at me for a while. I aim the camera at her and she asks, "Are you comfortable with it now? You look it." She stretches and she's about seven feet tall and I still can't get over how her hair sticks up.

She makes me want to know all of Ola's friends. I want to know who they are and what they've done. I'll put them all in front of the camera, and when the movie's done, it can be my gift to Ola. The other gifts I've given her are things she could put on the wall or wear. I figure this will be better than all that. I'll give her memories of her people.

Martha smiles at me after she stretches.

"David'll be home tomorrow. He's missed you."

Martha turns and walks away, in frame. She's halfway down the drive when I yell, "I've missed him too."

❦❦❦ CHAPTER 6

David sits next to my window at six o'clock in the morning, whistling. I know it is him 'cause I was with him the summer he learned how to do it. He's been whistling ever since. I roll over and ignore him for a while, but I can't wait to see him. David Two Starr is about as close as I get to having a brother. I guess that's why I know his whistle.

"You gonna sleep all day, Emmie?"

He's climbed in the window and is sitting at the foot of my bed trying on my hightops. David doesn't look sixteen; he looks the same as he did two years ago when I last saw him. His hair is down to his waist, and he has one blue eye and one brown eye.

David's lived with Martha Jackson since he was four years old. She's kept him longer than any other foster kid.

He lies down at the foot of the bed. "I got a new motorcycle, Emmie. It's a black racing bike, choice."

He starts tickling my feet. "I know you want to go for a ride, girl."

I do. I turn over and smile at the foot of the bed. "Hi, David," I say, then roll out to get some clothes. I find my jeans under the bed and a T-shirt on the dresser. I don't feel uncomfortable dressing in front of David. I used to take baths with him, and he's asking me where I found size one hundred tennis shoes, so I don't think he even notices.

David tosses the shoes in a corner, and I hop over them to get to the camera. He's already climbed out the window. I ignore my shoes and go out behind him.

"I left the bike by the road so I wouldn't wake anybody up." We run along the drive to the gate.

It *is* a choice bike. Beautiful. David leans against it. I hop on the back and put my helmet on before I see Mama sitting on the porch drinking coffee. She salutes us with her cup, and David takes off into the desert.

It's not all bright light in the early morning. The morning desert's a different place from the red-hot box that burns any part of your body it can get to. There's still oranges and purples in the sky. Mama says that it's toxic chemicals from Edwards Air Force Base, but I say it's beautiful.

David flies down the road. In an hour the dust will start blowing in and around. Now it's just the hum of the bike and the birds following us through the desert. We ride about twenty minutes when he yells back to me, "That's it, Emmie." He glides the bike to the side of the road and stops in front of an old ranch house, then sits back and stares ahead. I already have the video camera out. Martha says the batteries will last two hours.

"That's where your grandmother found us, Emmie. I guess I was four. My sister and brother were a little older. She'd bring us food we didn't have to cook. That's what Jeannie told me at least." David puts the kickstand down and leaves the bike.

I start walking down the long road to the house. It isn't really a road anymore. The desert has taken it back. David walks in front of me. I'd heard the story before about how Ola had come to get David and his sister and brother away from here.

"Dan and Jeannie told me they thought our father would be back, so every time the lady in the car with no top came to see us they'd say, 'Daddy's coming back in the night.' I don't know when she stopped believing them. I guess we started looking neglected or something."

We're at the house, and David is sitting on the steps now. At least he's sitting on what used to be steps, telling me that Martha sent him over this morning to help me out with the taping.

"I feel funny with that camera in my face, Emmie. Don't you feel strange going around with it?"

"No, not anymore."

"What do you want to know about your grandma that you can't ask her yourself?"

"I want to know what you remember about her when she found all of you out here. I want to know what you remember her looking like. Anything, David." I stop the camera and look at him running his hands across the steps. "Anything."

He gets up, walks over to a Joshua tree, and bends down for a stick lying beside it. "I know that she always drove by this way and she always drove up our road fast. Always thought that old Buick could really fly. I know she called me Baby until I'd tell her my name."

"How did she know you kids were here? You lived so far off the road. How'd she find you anyway? Nobody ever told me that part."

David starts to peel the stick and walks toward what used to be the living room window. It's lying by the tree too.

"Your grandma almost ran me down out there. Missed me by an inch. I can remember how the tires smelled when she picked me up out of the road."

I almost drop the camera. I don't believe it. Why didn't I know? I mean, it isn't a small thing to almost run over a kid in the desert. Ola never said a word about it. I'm not mad at her, though. I decide to be mad at David. I keep the tape going.

"Did you ever think about telling me my grand-mama almost killed you? Mama always talks about how Ola's going to mow somebody down one day in that car. Maybe you didn't remember it until a little while ago."

27

"I never forgot. You never asked, so I thought you knew about it. No big deal, Emmie."

I turn the camera off and start back to the road, kicking anything that gets in my way. The dust has started to blow. I don't know why finding this out now is so bad. It just is. I can almost see that big car coming at the little boy in the road. I can see Ola picking David up—her scarf blowing in his face and her dress getting dirty from his hands and the blowing dust.

I don't hear David running up behind me. If I had, I wouldn't have let him put his arm around me. I would have run to the road and ignored him when he got there. Now I have to knock his arm away.

Walk. Straight down the desert road, not even looking back. I hear David start the bike. I know he's going to follow me until I drop down dead. Lizards skitter from one side of the road to the other. I start whistling, and taping the lizards.

David glides behind me. I hear him. He doesn't have to talk.

It's not so reasonable, Emmie, to believe you know everything about everyone's life. So how can you be disappointed at something that happened so long ago? It had nothing to do with you. You're angry because you know you have no right to be angry.

And now you have to think about it. You've told me about how your mom and grandmother argue. You've always defended your grandmother, right? Always thought your mom was in the wrong about everything to do with her. One of the major things was your grandmother's wild driving. You always saw the driving as freedom from everything, but your mom saw it as plain dangerous. She was right, and now you're pissed.

Uh-huh. I stop the camera, turn, and smile at him. I put on my helmet.

If in your life you ever have a friend, it doesn't do to stay mad too long. I've never been angry at David before.

I get on the bike and hold tight as we race down the highway. I whistle when I can.

David drops me off where he picked me up. Mama is still sitting on the porch. She waves to him and goes back to reading the magazine on her knee. David takes my helmet and straps it onto the bike, then rides away saying he'll see me, and what about going to the mountains?

I walk up the drive and head toward Mama. I sit down by her feet and rub them. She smiles and looks down at me.

Both my parents are only children, so I was the first child that either one of them ever lived with. I started thinking about that 'cause I catch them staring at me, wondering what I'll do next. It's like they just discovered me off the coast of Lake Erie.

Sometimes it's good that they don't know what to expect or when to expect it. I didn't talk until I was almost three, but they weren't too worried. Ola said she was just about to send them Dr. Spock when I started talking in complete sentences and wouldn't shut up. They were saved a lot of worry.

Mama says they didn't have a clue about raising me. Since Ola lived thousands of miles away and my dad's parents were dead, there weren't any relatives around us to give them advice. Most of my parents' friends were just starting to have their own kids at the time, so they weren't any help.

Mama keeps reading, and I look at her feet that are shaped like mine.

ꝑꝑꝑ CHAPTER 7

Mama sits a little longer, enjoying her foot rub. When the flies start to buzz around us, she sends me in to help with the packing. I lean against the hall wall and see a box of pictures peeking out of the closet. They're pictures of Mama when she was three or four. In one picture she's sitting in front of a creek, holding a straw baby.

Ola comes in from outside, sweating. She stands by the screen door for a minute, then sits down beside me cross-legged. "That girl and her straw babies. Your mama loved straw babies as much as you did, Emmie. Your granddaddy would make them for her every time he thought about it. I'll teach you how to make them one day."

Ola stands up and walks away slowly. She says that she's getting arthritis and it has nothing to do with the cancer. She must have felt like I was looking at her 'cause she turns around and winks.

"Want to help?"

"Do what?"

"Anything," she says, and heads toward a stack of boxes in the kitchen.

I pick up the camera and follow her, remembering how much I had loved my own straw babies. I'd take bags of them home from the desert.

The noon sun pours through the kitchen window. Ola leans against the sink while the sun makes an aura around her—blue and warm. I hope the camera catches it—another part of her. For the first time in my life I really look at my grandmother. She's beautiful. Her dreads fall over her face when she moves and her skin glows from sweat. I hope the camera catches that too.

She washes the dishes while I pack up more napkins and tablecloths.

"David and I . . . talked about you a little . . . well, really a lot."

"About me, hmm." Ola shifts from one foot to the other, then turns around.

"When I lived in Alabama, Emmie, I never dreamed I'd live anywhere else in the world. I had your mother and I loved the man I thought I would spend the rest of my life with. I lived in a yellow house in a field, near my own mama. I was happy—had people that I loved and didn't know a damned thing about anything.

"When I came to the desert, I was running away from everything I had thought was safe and familiar.

This was another planet out here. A safer planet, but another planet. I don't think your mama ever forgave me for coming. She thought I'd lost my mind. I guess when you're fourteen and dragged across the country . . . "

"And sing Supremes songs all the time," I say.

"And have just lost your father," Ola says. She pauses. "There's nothing like violence and hate, Emmie. It's ugly and it never leaves you. Do you know what I mean?"

"No."

"Good, then. I hope you never have to know or feel it."

Ola walks to the screen door and looks out into the desert that stretches on forever. "Your granddaddy used to make those straw babies for your mother all the time. I got so sick of straw all around the house. I used to yell at him about it. That's the last thing I ever said to him, ya know: I yelled at him, when he was going out the door, to get all that straw out of the living room. I never saw him alive again. I hope you never get to see hate, baby."

Ola goes out the screen door and walks across the yard to sit under the Joshua tree. I keep taping her until I get a weak battery warning from the camera. I go back to the front hall and look at more pictures. Underneath some of Mama are pictures of my grandfather. In one of them he's standing by the old Buick that Ola drives now, and I remember the story.

All the photos I've seen of my mother's father are in black-and-white—so that's how I see him, my grandfather, in black-and-white. It must have been hot in Alabama, in the middle of July, but he's posing for a picture in the blazing sun, next to his new convertible. The picture shows him smiling, but I'm sure it wasn't a posed shot. He was probably smiling after the camera clicked and was put away. He was thirty-three when he could afford to buy his car.

Ola told me he'd saved to buy it since he was fifteen, but he didn't have a certain make in mind until he met her. She'd watched the movies and seen the beautiful people on the screen driving down coast roads in convertibles. They all wore dark glasses, and the women wore scarves that they slung back around their necks.

These people went to wonderful places in their cars. The places were freedom places, cafés with plants or long stretches of beach that said, "Take your shoes off and run into the water."

Of course, there weren't too many beaches on the gulf that they could drive to. It was unspoken that the beaches were "white only," but they could drive along the roads, so they did.

They were eighteen when they got married and pretty well sheltered from the rest of the world. They'd always lived in the country and knew who they'd known all their lives. My grandfather ran his father's farm. My grandmother kept the kids of the women who went into Montgomery to keep people's houses.

Mama said they never sat in at a lunch counter or went on any kind of civil rights march. She was always angry when she'd end by saying, "And they seemed happy anyway."

I think she blames their lack of attention to civil rights for my grandfather's death. She blames my grandparents' being happy with each other and living day to day. I've never heard her be angry at the people who sent threatening letters to them for being "uppity" and owning a brand-new car. I've never heard her scream and rage at the same people, who shot my grandfather by the side of his car and painted UPPITY NIGGER on the side of it.

Ola says Mama rages silently and bleeds inside. That's why she has a temper and would rather be angry than happy. Ola told her years ago that God was dead. Ola doesn't know what I know. My mama prays now. She prays in private. Maybe Mama isn't as angry as Ola thinks.

Maybe Mama has secretly forgiven the God that her own mama told her was dead.

When the sheriff looked into my grandfather's car, he found a bottle of milk, an Alabama road atlas, and a straw baby. The straw baby was for the baby my grandmother was supposed to have in seven months, but didn't. She lost it like she lost my grandfather. Suddenly and sadly.

My grandfather will smile forever beside the Buick convertible, but he will never be in living color for me. . . .

I walk back to the kitchen, and Ola is still sitting by the tree. I plug the camera into the outlet by the door. I tape Ola under the tree. In color.

%%% **CHAPTER 8**

I heard them early this morning. Far away—like a door closing two seconds before you're awake. You don't know if you've heard it. It could be head noises from waking up. I heard the aunts. The aunts always laughed. They'd be laughing when they came in the room, and laughing when they left.

I stretch and roll out of bed. If I stay in bed after 9:00 A.M. in the desert, I can't think clearly for the rest of the day. You have to get up before it gets hot. At nine it's already hot.

Walking across the room, I fall over clothes, boxes, and Thurmond, Ola's cat. Thurmond comes home when he's eaten all the lizards he can catch. He is wild. I dangle a T-shirt in front of him for a while and let him claw it. He doesn't have a tail and always manages to get locked in bathrooms. He eats all the toilet paper while he's there. I like him, but he soon gets tired of me and crawls under the bed.

I put on the T-shirt Thurmond has clawed and walk down the hall, camera in hand.

In the living room Mama is sitting on the floor in a pair of shorts. Ola's leaning back in the white wicker chair beside her. The aunts are all over the place.

They aren't related to us, the aunts. Everybody in Little Rock calls them that. Rachel, Margaret, Ruth, and Sara Title are sisters, and about two hundred and fifty years old collectively. At least, that's what Ola said a couple of years ago. I guess they've collected some years since I last saw them.

I love being near the aunts when they laugh and talk. I'm usually allowed to hang around and listen to grown people's talk when the aunts are around. The aunts would pass me from one to the other when I was little, braiding my hair, letting me sit on their laps while calling me "honey" and "sweet child" a lot.

I stand back in the cool of the hall shadows to get the room in focus. Mama, Ola, and the aunts come into view. In a second I see that Martha is there too. All that time I'd thought she was one of the aunts, Rachel maybe, but I spot Rachel at the stereo; their hairstyles are alike. Martha laughs with the rest of them and leans over to say something to Ola. Ola laughs and sips out of her mug. Mama traces patterns on the floor and around her feet, which are bare. She must be feeling better about being in the desert.

Everybody in the room listens to a story that Martha is telling them about Mama, and how they first met her and Ola. Sara pieces together a quilt. It lights up the room.

Ola will miss the aunts. Almost everybody she knows in the desert, she met through the aunts. If she didn't meet them through the aunts, they knew the aunts.

They've come to say a private good-bye, and to take Thurmond home to live with them. We locked him in last night so he'd be here. The aunts' good-bye is full of screams of laughter. So I watch, and I listen.

They talk of things I don't know about and some things that I do. Sliding down against the wall, out of sight, I watch them and tape them. When all the women are together, it's a party, a party without food and things to drink. It's a party without music. The only music is their voices.

This could be eavesdropping, but I don't think so. I could go into the room and tape everything that was said. No problem. They wouldn't mind, and I don't think that they'd pay too much attention to me and the camera. They're all used to it and me, but still I sit, listen, and look.

I listen to the sounds and move the camera from face to face. It's not important if that person is speaking or not. It's the faces of the women I want. These are the people who have loved my grandmother for years. Before me.

Ola worked for the state. That's how she met the aunts. They all worked for the state. I never knew what any of them did, except Ruth. I believe that she was one of the first women to work on a road crew. I think everyone else worked in offices. Anyway, when I'd get around to asking them what they did, they'd laugh and offer me food. So I stopped asking and decided that they were spies, 'cause I'd read Daddy's books about spies, and how you can't tell a spy by looking at one.

The old women in the room could never have been spies. Spies couldn't be happy, make quilts, can things, and garden. Would spies drive Jeeps into the desert to find old wagon wheels and talk about boyfriends who they say have been dead for years? I decide that they could, and am happy that I still like to think of them that way, mysterious and wonderful. They are all the people I'd ever read about in books. They smile and must know more than I ever will.

Ola is a secret woman too. She knows the aunts' stories and laughs uncontrollably sometimes, before the punch lines. I worry about taking Ola out of the desert, out of this place that she loves, this place of spies who quilt and have stories and secrets. I think I will feel older when she leaves here, no longer a spy, and me too old to believe anymore.

Ola says that the aunts are the desert to her. She says that they are wild and free, that they have to live in the desert. They couldn't be happy in the city or the suburbs. Ola says that she couldn't be happy in those places either, and I wonder how she's going to stand living with us.

I think Ola is so close to the aunts because they come from the South. They were born in the North, but moved south to start some sort of farm when they were in their twenties. They said they loved it there, but had to leave after fifteen years because people began moving too close to them.

The aunts wanted to leave for another reason too. The youngest of them had died from pneumonia the winter before they left. Her name was Grace Ann. The aunts took care of her for months. She'd suffered for a long time. You could tell the aunts still suffered about losing her. I could tell, because they'd get the same look in their eyes when they talked about her as Ola did when she talked about my grandfather. They still missed her.

I saw a picture of Grace Ann in the aunts' living room. She was beautiful and looked like she always smiled. If she had gotten older, she would have laughed all the time like her sisters. Ola said that my grandfather laughed all the time too. He smiled in his pictures, from the time he was a baby 'til he posed for the last picture with the Buick. I think all these things drew Ola and the aunts together.

In the living room now they are finishing each other's sentences and slapping their legs when the talk gets too funny. Margaret is handing iced tea around and teasing Sara about all the red fabric she's putting in the quilt. Ruth leans against Ola and they about fall over laughing.

Everything explodes into laughter. Ola lies down on the floor. Mama and Martha lean against each other and snort. But the aunts ... the aunts lose every bit of control they have and roll across the floor.

I lean back against the wall and take it all in. Thurmond walks down the hall toward me and starts to claw at my T-shirt. Everybody in the living room is still laughing. Thurmond looks in, raises his nose at all of them, and walks back down the hall to the bathroom.

CHAPTER 9

Last winter it rained a lot in the desert. Ola saved rainwater in barrels and talks about how much her plants love it. I haven't been lucky enough to see water coming from the sky. To me the sky above Little Rock only shoots out hot rays of heat and blinding light. To see rain in the desert . . .

I've never been to the desert in winter. I only know the summer. Ola says desert winters are different, at least this past year. Water was everywhere then, with everybody saying that the drought was over.

Ola's out back watering her plants now. They live in a greenhouse she made from a kit almost twenty years ago. She said she needed to see greens and reds.

Ola comes into the kitchen with a handful of cornflowers. She puts them in a jelly jar, then fills the jar up with water and puts it on top of the refrigerator. She's wearing a cotton housedress with daisies all over it. The yellow in the daisies bounces off her. She looks like a walking flower bed. She pulls up a chair and sits across from me and says between sips of iced tea, "Not too much time left to get packed up before the movers come. I didn't realize I had all this stuff, Emmie. I used to clean out my closets every two months. Where did it come from?"

I glance around at all the boxes in the kitchen. Most of them will be going to charity. I marked them.

Ola reaches across the table and runs her hand through my hair. I shaved most of it off before we came here.

"Are you thinking about growing dreads, my girl?" Ola winks.

"That's what I'm going for, but I don't know. I love to do other people's hair. I'm always cutting hair for my friends. Then their mothers are calling Mama to yell at her about me. I don't do anything to my own hair, though, except keep it really short."

Ola pulls hers away from her face until the corners of her eyes turn up. She leans back and closes them.

"I love the way my hair feels," she says. "I wake up in the morning, and it's there. All of it. I do wonderful things with it. I ignore it. I don't do wonderful things with it. The scarves are there. The hats are there. Hair should be kept at home—not loaned out to people who want to put strange objects and creams in it, then twirl you around in a chair and say, 'Marvelous, honey,' when you know your pets will be scared of you when you get back to the house."

I laugh and run my hand through my own hair. I never thought about my hair feeling good, but it does. I can't get all of it between my fingers, but I love the way the kinky waves feel. I decide then that I'll let my hair grow. I like the feel of it.

I didn't notice Ola leave the room, but a minute later she's coming back through the door with two boxes from somewhere else in this house of boxes. I take the one on top and put it on the floor. Ola sits down beside it, and I sit next to the other one.

The boxes are full of hats and scarves.

I used to go into Ola's room and spend the day there trying on every hat and scarf she had in the place. They were everywhere in her room. She had pegs on the walls and doors just for the hats and scarves. I'd daydream there for hours.

One minute I was an African queen with a tall crown of scarves, and the next day I was saving somebody from being eaten by sharks by throwing them a long silk scarf and pulling them out of the water.

Ola is digging through the box and pulling out a gold and silver scarf. She wraps it around my head until what little hair I have disappears underneath. Then she pulls a wide-brimmed black hat out of the box and tops off the scarf.

I find a yellow cotton scarf. I get up and stand in back of her. I pull her hair into a ponytail, then tie the scarf three times around it. Her ponytail stands straight up on her head. I used to fix her hair like that when she'd tell me she needed a change. At five I thought it was beautiful.

I close the kitchen door so we can look at ourselves in the mirror behind it. For the next couple of hours we try on everything in the box. It has to take a couple of hours because we started when the sun was about an hour from setting. When we're done, it's almost pitch-black outside.

Ola and I lie on our backs in the kitchen, scarves and hats everywhere. I look over at the night-light by the table. It's the only light in the room now. Ola's eyes are closed, but I don't think she's asleep.

I have always loved my grandmother, but I know that she is a strange woman. I know that not too many of my friends would spend an evening trying on hats with their grandmothers. A few years ago they would have. Now most of them don't even admit that they like their grandparents, though they do.

I'm clueless about how to be cool. I've always told my friends that I like my grandmother. Since most of them only get a glimpse of who she is by the books and strange things she sends through the mail, I think secretly they think she's cool. That makes up for me being clueless, I guess.

I look over at her again. She's singing a Supremes song into the air. She always sings when she's really relaxed. She sings before she falls asleep, and in the greenhouse. The thing is, she sings really loud. I think she forgets we're here sometimes. What drives me crazy, though, is waking up to her singing in the morning. I end up singing that song, whether I like it or not, for the rest of the day.

Ola stops singing and turns to me on the floor. "It'll all fall out, Emmie," she says. "I shouldn't be talking to you about this. . . . I think it's putting too much on you."

"I don't know what you're talking about," I say. "What's going to fall out?"

Ola starts to look at the night-light too. "My hair is going to fall out. It'll fall out in clumps when the chemotherapy starts."

She's never really said she wants chemotherapy. I think it's the first time she's mentioned anything about going to the hospital. Her talking about chemotherapy makes it all real. She's dying, and it feels real to me. Mama won't talk about it, and she wouldn't let Daddy talk about it either.

Ola sits up. "I've been thinking about it for a while. Somehow, I know I can't do it. My hair is my only vanity." Ola puts her hands in her hair. "I never thought of myself as a vain person, but all I can think of is, I don't want to lose my hair."

Ola leans against the kitchen chair for a minute, then lies down beside me again.

What can I say? I can't say anything. I just keep looking at the night-light. Ola put it there when I was four years old. I was a night wanderer then. She was afraid I'd break my neck in the dark. She put night-lights all over the house to make me feel safe. I don't feel safe anymore.

I try to deal when grown people are losing it around me. I don't do it very well, though. I still go to my room and cover my head when Mama and Daddy yell at each other. I don't watch the news anymore. I can never get credit in my government class when we have to discuss current events. I saw the news during the Gulf War and I haven't watched TV since.

Mama says I should toughen up about some things. I am tough about what's important. I can take the train downtown by myself. I can stay alone in our apartment overnight.

I reach for Ola's hand. It's cold. We hold hands until hers warms up and mine starts to feel cool. We both lie on the floor staring straight up. My stomach starts to growl.

I look over at Ola just as her face breaks into a grin. She says, "It's a wonder both of us don't pass out from hunger right on this floor. How about beans and rice?"

I get up and go to the light switch. When I flip it, the sun seems to have flooded through. Ola is sitting cross-legged on the floor, rubbing her eyes. She looks around the kitchen and shouts, "Oh, child, look at this kitchen. It looks like a hat store blew up in here." She starts putting everything back in the boxes. I climb up on the cabinet over the sink to get to the rice.

Ola picks everything off the floor and table and takes the boxes out of the kitchen. I hear her laughing a second after she's left. I don't turn around, though, or I'd fall off the countertop. I move all the cans out of the way and finally find the rice, then jump backward to the floor. This is something that would have Mama screaming in fits if she saw me do it.

"You're going to break every bone in your body doing that, girl."

I turn to find Mama sitting at the kitchen table. She has the video camera aimed right at me. She's got her bare feet propped up on the tabletop and she's wearing one of Ola's old straw hats. I take a bow. Mama smiles and walks out of the kitchen, saying something about recharging the batteries.

I say, "I charged them earlier, Mama, and I haven't used the camera since."

Mama comes back into the kitchen and looks at me for a long time, then says, "I wish she felt she had me, baby, but I'm glad she has you." She puts the old straw hat on my head and leaves. I pull the hat closer to my head and run the water in the pot to boil the rice.

❦❦❦ CHAPTER 10

Mama talks. . . .

When she was younger, Emmie hated leaving the desert. It was no good warning her beforehand that vacation was almost over and we'd be going home to her daddy in a few days. Telling her only made it worse. She'd take time out to cry about it for at least two hours every day before we actually left.

She'd crawl up on my lap and beg to stay with her Ola, because her grandmama would miss her, she would miss David, and there weren't any mountains near Cleveland, et cetera.

So I took to telling her we were leaving the day of our return flight. It was hard and, I have to say, some things you just don't forget. I'll never forget her hands in her mouth and the low moan before the real crying would start. There was nothing anybody with any sense could do. Ola and I would leave her in the room where she'd found out the bad news and go on about our business.

I'd get together what I didn't have packed, hoping it was in some other part of the house, far away from Emmie's crying.

Ola would go sit out on the kitchen porch with some iced tea, then head for the greenhouse. She'd start singing. It would get louder and louder; then Emmie's crying would get louder too. I used to make bets with myself about which one would be the first to drive me crazy. It's still a mystery to me how my mother's voice could carry so far out of that greenhouse.

I guess Emmie's crying would carry into it, so to be fair, I suppose Ola had to fight back. In a few minutes, though, Emmie would stop.

By chance, every time she'd find out we were leaving, she'd have on her only dress. She'd have on her tennis shoes and baseball cap too. The hem of the dress would always end up in her mouth, and her dress would be soaked with tears. She'd drag herself into the front room and sit in the middle of the floor. I guess she didn't want anyone to get out the front door without knowing that they had just messed up what was left of her summer.

I took a picture of Emmie the August she was eight years old, sitting in the middle of the living room. She looked miserable and lonely after finding out we were leaving that evening. When I got the film developed a week later and saw her face, I knew that picture was unfair, and that I shouldn't have taken it. All that unhappiness was private in its own way. All the crying and acting up was something she had to do to get over it.

I found out when Emmie was older that she couldn't remember the fits and that her grandmama didn't remember them as any big deal. I figure it was all in my head.

I never liked the desert, and here was a child of mine crying to stay. What was wrong with her? Worse, she was crying to stay with the woman whom I love but have never understood. I left the desert and my mama when I was seventeen years old and angry. One morning I told Ola I was moving to San Francisco. She stared at me for a few seconds before she started packing me a bag of fruit for the trip.

She was as tired of fighting as I was when she put me on the Greyhound going north. When the bus took off, I pressed my face against the window and cried. Ola followed that bus for five miles down the dusty desert road. She gave me every chance to change my mind and stop the bus, but I didn't.

When I got an address in San Francisco and quit having so much fun walking through the city, I wrote Ola to say how wonderful it all was. Haight Ashbury, the record store I got a job at, and the house where I lived with twelve other people. She crocheted me a poncho and stuck in a scarf. I wore both of them to a party the day I got them, and thought about my mother, but not about the desert.

I crisscrossed the country over the next ten years, and Ola still sent me things through the mail. Food, clothes, and money would get to me when I was just about to ask for them. In ten years I went back home only twice. I thought about my mama a lot, but the memory of the place we had run to after my daddy died didn't make me happy.

After a while I found a man I thought I could love forever, and I do. I took him to the desert. When we had Emmie, I took her there too.

Emmie doesn't feel a prisoner on the desert, torn away from another world, like I had been—an ugly world, but mine nonetheless. There's no reason for her to feel panic here. The desert for her is David, and the mountains in the distance. The desert is the aunts and their strange ways. The desert is her grandmama, hats, and an old Buick Electra flying down all the back roads.

I sit outside the kitchen now, watching my daughter and her grandmama cook beans and rice for dinner. They move together and are easy with each other in close quarters. I know that after I was fourteen I was never easy with Ola. She was easy with me, though, when she let me go looking for something that I have long since forgotten.

Emmie doesn't have the fits anymore when it's time to go. Of course, time would take care of that. Now she's the one who picks up the plane tickets from the travel agency around the corner from us in Cleveland. She knows when we leave and when we come back. She knows the seat numbers and reminds me to order her a vegetarian meal for the plane.

The day before we leave her grandmama's house, she tears through the desert with David and says good-bye to everyone. The evening before we leave, she and Ola walk into the desert near the house. They talk for hours, two dots in the distance, wearing hats.

When Ola drives us to the airport the next day, scarf flying in the wind down the California freeways, Emmie looks at the scenery. When we get to the airport, she hops out of the car to find our gate and buy gum.

All the last good-byes and hugs are done and we're on the plane; it's then, and only then, that she'll press her face against the window and cry.

🐚🐚🐚 **CHAPTER 11**

Ola says she'll teach me to drive the Buick before we leave for Ohio, but I'm way ahead of her. I've taken the car out twice and driven it a little way down the road—past the convenience store near the crossroads.

I'm doing it again tonight.

The first time I took Ola's car was a couple of nights ago, after the aunts had left. It was about two in the morning when I looked in on Ola. Her bedroom light was on, but she had fallen asleep reading. Mama was still up in the back bedroom, packing papers and books. She had the radio on and was in another world.

I got the keys off the hook in the hall and sneaked out the front door, trying not to feel guilty about doing what I was about to do. Mama's voice was screaming in my head:

"Stealing is stealing and there ain't no way around it."

She'd said that when I'd stolen a dog from one of our neighbors. I didn't think they were treating him right, he was so skinny. But in the end I had to take him back. It was stealing, Mama said. I called it rescuing. I was trying to make myself believe I was taking the car so Ola wouldn't have to be bothered so much about teaching me to drive.

I'm sticking with that if I get caught.

Anyway, David really taught me how to drive two summers ago. Martha had an old station wagon that hadn't been crashed yet by the kids. David didn't have a license, but Martha had taught him how to drive when he was twelve, and he was going to teach me.

Martha came with us on a hot morning that July. We pulled out of her driveway and headed for a long stretch of road going toward the mountains. She sat in the back with a Walkman listening to meditation tapes and looking relaxed, considering. She said she was going for the ride and to make sure we didn't get arrested.

An hour later—I was twelve and driving.

Driving the old station wagon through the brush.

Driving it down an old road that dead-ended at a water tower.

Driving in circles around the Joshua trees that dot the desert around Little Rock for miles.

Martha and David found an old shed and watched me from the top of it. Not once did I see either of them jump off the shed and run toward me, trying to save my life.

The station wagon was quiet. It went all over the brush, an old tire, and a lot of other things people had dumped in the open desert with hardly a sound.

I had a few more lessons. I even drove on the road with other cars and did fine. David would sleep in the back, and Martha would sit in the front when I was in traffic. The second week of lessons, though, one of the kids wrecked the station wagon. It'd be another two years before I'd drive again.

It was the pills beside Ola's bed that put me in mind to practice driving before Ola's lessons.

The house had started looking like a warehouse. Mama was always on the phone to the movers or the real estate agent who's going to find a renter for the place.

Ola was packing, tending the greenhouse, and talking about having a yard sale. I'd been running around with the camcorder looking for something or someone to tape. I helped with the packing when somebody asked me. I was getting good at marking boxes wrong and had given away a box of dishes by mistake.

Mostly I taped Ola and talked to her while she packed. There's hours of quiet in the tapes. If I sat down without the camera, though, Ola would say, "Not filming today, sister?" and smile.

A couple of days ago I couldn't find anything to do

and didn't have the camera, so I started wandering through the house. Most of the closets were empty. Mama had torn through them like she had only a minute. Looked like she'd have everything packed up in about another hour. I figure she could get a job doing this and forget about teaching part-time at the college, which is all she says she can stand.

I soon wandered into Ola's room.

She has the coolest room in the house. If there is a breeze, it comes through this room. Her walls are yellow, and the curtains too. They blow in the slightest breeze. Ola has a white cotton spread on her bed and an Indian rug she got from Martha on the floor. I looked for the vase of flowers—she always has flowers—and found it on a table by the window.

This was my nap room when I was little. I touched the flowers, the rug, then stopped wandering and stretched out on the bed. I traced the designs on the spread. I watched the ceiling fan for a while, then ran my fingers to the edge of the spread, to Ola's nightstand.

I counted eight bottles of pills on the nightstand beside the wishing well lamp. I started reading labels. Two said As Needed for Pain. I dropped one of the bottles on the floor and rolled to the other side of the bed.

I couldn't think of my grandmama in pain. I didn't want to think of her in pain, so I thought about every kind of pain I'd had in my whole life. A broken leg, stitches in my chin, tonsils out. I didn't think I'd ever be out of pain when I was in it.

Ola's pain would be with her as long as she lived. Ola's pain took pills to make it go away, a different kind of pain, something Band-Aids couldn't fix.

I thought of Ola picking us up at the airport, laughing and packing boxes—telling me what was in them. Was she in pain then? Could she even be out of bed if it weren't for the pills? Mama sometimes says that she can't do anything when she has a headache. God.

Ola wanted to give me driving lessons before she gave the car to Martha. When she told her that she could have it, I don't think Martha really believed her. Martha kept saying, "Get out of here." Then she started to laugh. She said yes in the end—went right home and told all the kids that they'd wrecked the last car belonging to her. I doubt she'll let even David drive that Buick.

Here I am. Stealing my grandmama's car in the dark, putting it in neutral and letting it roll down the hill in the driveway. I can't turn the lights on until I hit the road. That's what I do, then try to remember everything David taught me. There's nobody on the road this time of night, and I'm gone.

It's cool now, but I let the top stay down 'cause I like the way the night air feels all over. I can't see the desert or the mountains—not too many streetlights out here. I'm going about thirty, and have just passed the only gas station in Little Rock, when I know why I love the desert. I know why Ola loves the desert, and why Mama says she used to hate it. It's the quiet. It's a good place not to hear anything if you don't want to hear it. I hear the wind, though, as I drive past the crossroads.

I pull to the side of the road after a while, to practice parallel parking with two rocks that I find. I do okay. I lie on top of the hood. An old song that Mama sometimes sings comes on the radio, and I get off the car and start dancing into the headlights. As I watch a lizard stare into the headlights, then take off, I think about taking the car back. I stay a little longer, though, waiting for something besides me to dance into the light.

༒༒༒ CHAPTER 12

Ola asks me in the morning, at breakfast, how my driving lessons are going. Mama's leaning against the table, drinking coffee.

"Well, my girl, you going to answer your grand-mama?"

I just look at them. They look at me and start laughing. I figure they knew all about me taking the car the whole time.

"She rides real smooth, don't she, baby? Never given me any trouble at all. I keep her tuned."

I take Mama's coffee out of her hand. "Does she really have only twenty thousand miles on her, Ola? That car's old."

Ola goes over to the window, looks out, and says, "Twenty thousand is all she has on her. It's not the age—it's how you take care of the aged. And before I forget, your dad called this morning. He told me he missed both you and your mama. Couldn't wait to see all of us. He also asked if you wanted an iguana."

Mama looks at Ola. I guess she thinks Ola got the message messed up. "An iguana?"

"Oh, yeah, I do."

"Why do you want an iguana?"

"I've always wanted an iguana, Mama."

"You never said anything to me about it, but, hey, you've been driving for some time, it seems, and I didn't know about that either. Did anybody mention the picnic in the hills to you yet? The aunts and half of Little Rock will be there."

Ola says, "That oughta fill half a van. You going, Emmie?"

"No, I thought I might steal everybody's cars while they're at the picnic—then sell 'em for parts."

"Hmm, a smart-ass. Well, I got something for you. Do you think you could get a few boxes packed? They're already marked. All the things that go in them are right beside the boxes."

"You trusting me?"

"I always trust you. I mean as long as you don't give the stove or anything else away. I'll be cool."

"Where you going that you're trusting me with your house?"

"I got a doctor's appointment, and your mama's coming with me. We won't be long."

"I'll be okay for a couple of hours. After that I might get the urge to start losing things or to give heavy furniture to people who are just passing by. So you better hurry back."

In a few minutes Mama and Ola are gone.

Ola's room is still cool. It must never get hot in here. A couple of bottles are missing from the nightstand. I sit on the bed and read the labels on the ones that are left. Both the bottles of pain pills are gone. One more bottle is missing too. Maybe the pills aren't working. That idea makes me feel sick, so I start for the back room to pack the boxes Ola's left for me.

It's mostly old clothes and books. I can't believe Ola ever wore clothes like this; some of the dresses look like they're made from scarves. Most are back in style now. They're short enough. The colors are pretty scary though, so I hurry up and put them in the box so I'll be safe.

Most of the books are little kids' picture books and coloring books. Must have been on the back room shelves all these years. The books look too old even to belong to Mama. The boys are all wearing cowboy hats, and all the girls are having tea parties, but I look through them anyway. . . . Ola must save everything. Mama always says the opposite; she says she used to have to chase the garbage man all the time— Ola was always throwing something of hers away.

When one of the books comes apart in my hand, I know why Ola has kept it and all the rest. A little kid has written his name in the corner of the cover.

Charles Lundon Werren. Ola kept all my grand-daddy's books. They must have been about all she brought from Alabama after he died.

I open each one and read it three or four times.

I love the coloring books best. My grandfather colored everything strange colors. I think he was old enough to know the right ones, and he colored beautifully, stayed in the lines—which is something I always thought was stupid to do. Even so, horses were green, the sky was red. The people in the book were never colored. He left them the way he found them.

Ola kept books from when he was older too, and letters. They'll all fit in the one box that Ola has marked CHARLES'S THINGS.

I start missing a man I never knew, a man who colored horses green and got letters from someone called Carl. I guess it's okay to read letters. It's not like I knew this Carl; Mama might think differently, though.

My granddaddy must have known Carl for a long time 'cause some of the letters talk about them being kids together. Granddaddy was married when Carl wrote him 'cause Carl always mentions Ola, and a little later somebody he calls Little Bit. That must be Mama.

Most of the letters are funny. Sometimes I can't understand them, 'cause I don't have Granddaddy's letters back. They must have cared about each other 'cause Carl's letters always ended *Bye, Buddy. Love, Carl.*

I think about my friends, whom I miss and haven't seen in a while. I think about people whom I only met a couple of times and never saw again. I even think about people whom I see every day and have never met.

I almost never think about my granddaddy. Seems strange never to think about someone who was so close to people I love. Mama doesn't talk about him, 'cause I think it still hurts so much. Ola talks about him like he's still living sometimes. She never will get over him. But me, if I think about him twice a year, that's good.

A lady who lives down the hall from us in Cleveland tells fortunes and always talks about ghosts. Minnie Jacobs. She says the reason people talk about dead people they loved, like they were still here, is because they probably still are. She says when somebody dies in an accident or suddenly, their souls just stay here. It's better if someone knows you're dying; then people are around to tone the sweep.

She says when she was a little girl in South Carolina and someone died, a relative would get a hammer and hit a sweep, a kind of plow, to let everybody know. She always believed you had to do it right after to ring the dead person's soul to heaven. I don't know about heaven, but she got me thinking about restless souls, and I wonder if my granddaddy could be one of them.

Mama calls Ola a restless soul. She said restlessness is the reason she left Alabama the day of Granddaddy's funeral. She said that's why Ola moved to a place where there was so much space. She'd have enough space to roam in the desert.

Ola calls Mama a restless soul 'cause she's lived all over the country and had about twenty jobs in the last ten years.

I don't know if I'd call either of them restless. Maybe hyperactive about some things. Anyway, I think as long as your soul is still attached to your body, it's impossible for it to be restless. I think you go where your spirit takes you.

Maybe Granddaddy really is here, since he doesn't have a body now. I hope he is, for Ola. If he's here, I think she'd know it. I start to imagine he's in the room wondering who I am—going through his old books and letters—and decide it's time to finish packing the box and go into the heat outside.

I wait for Mama and Ola on the front porch, drinking cold water and thinking about Granddaddy and thinking how I miss Daddy now. He told me that all we are is soul—most of us. I want to believe it. If you believe that, then when people die and are buried, you'll never miss them. You can sit and think about them. Your heart will never hurt for them, 'cause all they ever were was soul.

Mama and Ola pull into the driveway and wave. Ola gets out of the car slowly and walks to the porch. She sits down quietly beside me. I put my arm around her. Mama sits down too and leans against the porch. She hums a song that I remember her singing to me when I was little.

Ola asks about packing and if there were any phone messages. I tell her nobody called and the packing went fine.

I woke up a minute ago from a dream. It's pitch-black in my bedroom, and I can feel a breeze coming in from my window. In my dream I'm Mama. I'm sitting in an old car—sitting in the road really. I'm waiting for someone who never comes. Even though I don't know who I'm waiting for, I cry for them.

My face is still wet from the dream when I get up to look out my window.

ಌಌಌ **CHAPTER 13**

Ola decided at the doctor's office yesterday that she wasn't going through with the chemotherapy. Mama isn't talking.

The only reason I can see that Ola is moving to Cleveland is to get well at the hospital there, but now she says she's coming to be close to us while she's dying. She told Mama that—really she screamed it— so I couldn't help hearing it. Mama kind of sank to the chair and said she knew that Ola would pull something like this.

Ola keeps telling her that she's said all along she wasn't sure about a cure that was going to make her so sick, when the doctor gave her only a 10 percent survival rate anyway. Mama starts crying, and that's when I jump off the back porch and make the walk to David's house.

I find him under his bike. He keeps it tuned, I guess, by living under it.

I hand him tools for about twenty minutes. We don't say anything to each other until I can't hold it in.

"They're both crazy, you know."

David sits up and tightens something on the wheel. I hand him a wrench. "Who's crazy?"

"My mother and my grandmother, who else? Who do I spend my time with? Who else would I be talking about?" Then I start crying and have to go sit on his porch. David scoots around and looks at me for a minute on the porch, but that only makes me cry harder so I get up and go in the house.

Dan and Jeannie are visiting and watching the kids while Martha is in L.A. They go to college in Northern California and hardly talk, like David. They're watching a gourmet cooking show and smile at me when I sit down in the middle of the floor and watch with them.

David comes in a few minutes later and washes up. When he's pretty sure I won't cry again, he sits next to me and puts his arm around my neck.

"Still think both of them are crazy, Emmie?"

"Yes."

"Why?"

"Because they both make me crazy when they fight."

"Then leave when they fight."

"I'm here, aren't I?"

David flips through the remote, and Dan and Jeannie don't seem to mind. "What's the problem, then? When they fight, leave. When they aren't fighting, stay. Does it have anything to do with you?"

"No."

"Good, 'cause people are going to do just what they want to do, and feel the way they want to, with or without you. Get used to it."

David hauls himself up and goes to the kitchen to feed the kids, who have been whining for about ten minutes. I don't know most of them. Sometimes Martha only keeps them for a week or two. Sometimes she has them for years.

Nothing freaks David too much. He's lived with so many kids for so long he can take anything. I nod toward the door that I'm leaving, and he waves a peanut butter sandwich at me. Dan and Jeannie smile again when I say bye. They're watching an Italian racing car documentary now.

I walk back toward Ola's.

Mama still isn't talking. Ola isn't bothered about anything. She's going on about visiting an old friend and about how she needs a break from packing. She packs tomatoes in a bag and wraps cut flowers in wet newspaper. She says her friend paints. I put the video camera in its case when she invites me along. When we leave, Mama is reading a book.

We pick up Martha, who's just gotten back from L.A. She talks about how she hasn't been there since the riots. And both talk about how the violence made them sick.

Then they talk about the friend who paints—Roland—and how they met him. Martha's kids plowed into his car at the grocery store, "but everybody's been friends ever since."

I sit listening and gulping water as Ola flies through the desert. I've taken to carrying water with me. It's gotten so hot. The heat's sucking all the water out of me. Doesn't look like it bothers Ola and Martha. They talk on.

We pull over to the side of the road so Ola can take a pill. I think it's a pain pill 'cause Martha looks concerned, and she's never really concerned about anything. Ola drinks out of my water bottle and says she's all right. She gets behind the wheel again and doesn't mention the pill.

Roland's house is built into a hill. Right into a hill. I like it and him before he comes running off the porch to meet the car and us with a tray of ice water.

Roland could be anywhere from forty to sixty. He's the same height as Martha, bald, and wearing a gray sweatshirt with a tree on the front of it. Roland is a hugger and makes sure he doesn't miss anybody. He has a nice smell of paint and cookies on him.

Martha, he, and Ola go into the house. They haven't paused for breath since we got out here and don't notice that I'm not following them.

I have to duck under vines to get into Roland's backyard. I didn't think vines like this could grow in the desert. They're so green. So green.

I rub my arms into the vines and sit in them until I'm sure what I hear is water running. I get up and walk through the vines that end on a patio made of stones. The hill drops water into a pond twenty feet from Roland's house. The vines block out most of the sun, so the patio floor is cold when I sit down. I put my feet in the water and listen to it falling, and think I could stay here forever.

I dream. I am swimming one minute, and the next I'm watching my dad paint our extra room yellow for Ola. Everything smells like lemon and flowers in the room, and we all sit around talking about how Ola will like it. Ola has her back to us, looking out the window. She never turns around. I start thinking it isn't her at all— Then I wake up. A large dog has his head on my stomach. I must be in his spot. He doesn't look like he's minded sharing, so I stay a few more minutes, then go looking for everybody.

I remember the camera and go back to the car. I record the vines, the green. I go through a sliding glass door in the back and end up in the kitchen with all three of them sitting around drinking iced coffee. The dog follows me in. I record Roland.

Roland leans back in his chair. "Did you like the pond? I was lucky to find this house. It was falling down when I found it. Looked like an old miner's shack."

"It doesn't feel real. What happened to the desert back there?"

"I get the water from the snow in the mountains. It's been incredible this year—all the rain."

Roland pours me a cup of coffee. It tastes like cinnamon and is ice-cold. I sit down at the table with the rest of them and pan the camera to the patio. I could watch the water pour down the hill all day long.

I ask, "What's the green vine growing in the back?"

Roland smiles at Martha and Ola. He looks surprised too. "Hasn't your grandmother ever told you about kudzu? It's hers, you know. She grows it in her greenhouse and has to keep the other plants safe from it. She brought it with her from Alabama and gave me some when she saw where I lived."

Ola says, "Where I come from in Alabama, people hated it. It grows overnight and takes over crops, houses, trees. You can go down the highway and see fields and woods covered in the stuff. I always made believe that I hated it when I was there, but I loved it. Something no one could stop."

Martha scratches the dog on the head. Roland tells me his name is Jake. "Your grandma . . . ," he says. "A while ago she threatened to give me some of that plant. Said I'd be able to grow it with water and sunlight, but I had nightmares about waking up in the morning with it all over the house, eating the kids and the refrigerator."

"Why did you bring it to California, Ola?"

"It was something from where I used to be, Emmie. It can't talk about Alabama or take me back, but it reminds me. I think the state of California wouldn't want it here; it's considered a pest. But maybe we don't have to worry about it attacking too much in the desert."

Roland offers me more coffee and then leaves the room.

I say, "I like him."

Ola looks out at the waterfall. "He's a gentle man."

Martha cracks, "And not afraid of vicious plant life."

"He's painted a picture of me. . . . He asked for some time. So a few months ago I sat for some sketches. He made do with those, I guess. I never wanted even my picture taken 'til a while ago. I used to run from cameras and people with sketch pads."

Roland comes back with a canvas covered by an old cotton shirt. He sets it up on the table after we've cleared the cups away. He uncovers Ola.

She's the woman I remember when I was about two. A yellow-flowered loose dress and flowing scarf blow in the wind. She's barefoot and laughing, with flowers at her feet, leaning against her car. You can see one eye from underneath her hat, and it's laughing.

We all sit looking at the painting, not saying anything.

Ola takes the bag of tomatoes from under the table and gives them to Roland.

"Beautiful, Roland," she says.

He bows like somebody out of an old movie and hands the painting to her. We get up to leave.

Martha reminds Roland about the picnic, and we climb into the Buick and then wave to him and Jake until they're out of sight. In a few minutes the house living in the hillside is gone, disappeared from camera view, and we're driving through the desert again.

I sit in the front passenger seat while Martha drives. Ola falls asleep in the backseat beside the painting, her scarf blowing in the wind.

❦ ❦ ❦ CHAPTER 14

The first time I ever went to the Highway Store, I was three years old. Ola drove me and David there as the sun was going down. I remember an orange glow on the white seats. David sat next to me. Our feet stuck out in front of us, and we chose candy dots, on paper, for our treat.

Miss Sally Hirt owns the Highway Store, then and now. When I'd come back to the desert for vacations, she'd call down to the house for me. Says I remind her of her granddaughter whom she doesn't get to see so much.

When Miss Sally calls from the store this time, I go with the camera. I ride on the back of David's bike and think about how different it all is from the first time I came here. The store hasn't changed. Fruit still sits outside in baskets and garden tools lean against the front wall. I've changed. I've become a regular person.

That's what Miss Sally calls anyone who can speak in complete sentences.

She said on the phone that she wanted to talk about Ola 'cause she heard I was asking Ola about Miss Sally. That's enough for her. She'd tell me anything she could, she said, and laughed about wanting to be on television.

I sit on the back of the bike after David puts the kickstand down, pull off the lens cap, and tape the outside of the store. It's an everything store. You can get groceries and tires in the same aisle.

Miss Sally Hirt's face shines when I walk through the door. She's what Ola calls a big-boned woman. She keeps her hair pulled back in a bun, but says, when I walk in, that she might take it down for me, 'cause it goes to her knees.

David sits on a high wooden stool beside me and looks through catalogs piled up by the register. I pan the camera around the store and think about Mama shopping here when she was my age—buying junk food and bottles of pop.

"You children hungry?" Miss Sally yells from the back. She brings out a bowl of fruit and iced tea. "I heard somewhere that both of you are vegetarians. Why is it that young people don't want to eat meat anymore?"

David looks up, shrugs, and smiles.

I shrug with the camera in my face and point it at steaks under glass in the deli section.

"You know, you look so much like your mama it's almost a mirage. She came in for the first time the day after they'd moved here. Her eyes were big, and she looked like she hadn't got a good night's sleep in a while. Ola looked refreshed, though. She came bustling in after your mama and bought their groceries for the week. I liked her accent. What I really remember about them, though, is your mama looking like she'd walked from Alabama and your grandma looking real refreshed—like she'd been freed from something."

I bit into an apple. "What do you think Ola'd been freed from?"

"Well, like everybody, I know what happened to your poor grandfather. I guess all the strain just left her when she was finally settled somewhere else."

I focus in on her face. It's round and burned from the desert sun. When she smiles, all the lines smile too.

"But the strain sure showed on your mama's face. She was so young to have gone through something so bad. She hated it here. Just looked like she'd never come out of it. You know, they didn't get help for people back then—trauma and all."

A customer comes in, and Miss Sally leaves the counter to help him.

David leans over toward me. "Top-of-the-line computer," he says, and holds a catalog out to me. I look at it for a minute and realize I wouldn't know top-of-the-line if it hit me.

Miss Sally rings up the man's order.

"And her finding him like that." She stops suddenly and looks real pained. David looks up and puts the catalog down. It's easier for me not to move. If I stay real still, nothing will happen; the past will not have happened. If I can just hold my hands still and keep the camera from shaking.

Miss Sally leans over the counter but draws back when she notices I haven't moved. Not one inch. She can't hold my hand or take back what she's said. It's not her fault that I didn't know.

"I guess it's not something your mama wanted to tell you about. Well. . . . I guess she was out in the woods fishing with some of her friends and they decided to take the road back. . . ."

Now I know where Mama's anger comes from. It all falls into place: why Mama hated Little Rock and had weeks of quiet times and didn't talk about Granddaddy very much. It was a relief to know why she was sad sometimes. I kind of understood why she was mad at Ola a lot too. Ola was hurt, but it didn't run as deep as Mama's hurt.

Miss Sally talks on about how she'll miss Ola 'cause she's a good card player and a good friend. She tells some jokes and gets David laughing. After a while I start laughing too. . . .

When we leave Miss Sally Hirt's store, she takes her hair out of its bun. It does go down to her knees. She waves us away.

David takes me to the hills outside of Little Rock to climb. There's a point where you can see the entire valley. It's beautiful. It makes me so sad to think I may not see it for a long time. I can't see Mama spending the money to send me here in the summers if Ola isn't here.

We climb to the top of the hill, then start to hike the trail down it. A creek twists around the bottom; we can hear it from the top of the hill. I can't wait to put my feet in the cool water below.

David and I sit in the creek for a couple of hours. Leaves float by, and we lean back on the rocks and look up at the sky.

David never asks me how I feel. I asked him once why. He said my feelings were my own, nobody else's. Nobody's business. I'm glad he feels like this. I guess I'm like Mama that way. I don't share my feelings too much. At least with David, he feels *for* me. That's enough.

Mama comes into my room when I'm just about to go to sleep. I scoot over and let her in the bed.

"You having a good time here, Emmie?"

I find Mama's hand in the dark and squeeze real hard.

"I talked to Miss Sally today, Mama. I taped her. I think she was into it. . . ."

"She called and told me, baby."

I say, "Yeah," and squeeze her hand tighter, then move over so she can have more room. She's asleep before I am as the curtains blow in the night breeze.

CHAPTER 15

The next night I slept outside, in the desert by the house. Got a blanket from one of the boxes that's going to a shelter in L.A. Most of the night I was okay, but I dreamed the rest of the time. I don't dream so much in Ohio.

I've started seeing boxes in my sleep, then pictures of Joshua trees along winding roads that can't be out in the desert.

And I dream of Ola driving down a road. I'm standing on the side, and she always passes me by. . . .

The first time I had that dream, I was afraid to tell Mama and I didn't know why. I thought I'd stay up so I didn't have to go back to it. But that didn't work. I tried to wake myself in the middle. I couldn't.

I finally told her about the dreams yesterday when she was moving furniture around in the living room. She listened for a while and said if they really bothered me that much, I could sleep with her. I thought about it. I didn't tell her that's not what I wanted. I wanted her to make them stop, and I felt dumb for even thinking it.

That's when I got the idea about sleeping out in the desert. Everybody always says fresh air helps you sleep. I was starting to think it was the house that wasn't letting me sleep. All the boxes had too many things in them, and there was too much going on in the daytime. The house wasn't resting, so I couldn't.

The time was getting close. It was so close. In a couple of days we'd be gone. In the beginning, packing hadn't bothered me. Now it was like closing up everything I knew and had cared about. I was being smothered by old books and towels that a week ago were just things. Now they were things that other people would find a use for. It would no longer matter that my grandmama had ever made use of them.

I found a clearing with no brush. I stayed close enough to the house to hear the window fan in the front room. It didn't take long before I was out cold.

I must have slept, 'cause when I started dreaming this time, I wasn't going through the dream so tired.

Ola drove by me again in the car. This time I chased her down the road. Just when I thought I could catch her, the car was gone. I dreamed some more, but can't remember any of it. I woke up not knowing where I was for a few seconds, then sat up in the desert and looked at the dark house.

I got my blanket and walked back to the porch. Mama was sitting in the corner of the porch in her pajamas and a sweater.

"Wouldn't have done you too much good to sleep with me anyway. All night I've been right here."

I sat down by her, leaned against the house, and thought that she's going to miss the desert and she doesn't even know it yet.

She looked at me and said, "Too many boxes." I covered us with my blanket; then I fell back to sleep.

And now it's morning.

❦❦❦ CHAPTER 16

Martha says she's going to dance at the picnic. She says she hasn't danced in years but has found some music that she really likes. She thinks it's some kind of chanting about fertility, but she's not sure. Ola says she shouldn't take any chances with so many people of childbearing age around. Mama sits back and laughs.

We've packed the last of the boxes up. Now all anybody is worried about is whether the movers will get here on time. We separated the furniture this morning. It's sitting around in different parts of the house waiting for somebody to load it into a van, sell it, or give it away. Ola decided that any furniture she had, made of wood, she'd give to her friends, and the rest of it would go to a consignment shop.

I see Ola sitting in the backyard under the Joshua tree, her favorite place. The phone's been ringing most of the morning, and she's probably tired of it.

Since I haven't been able to sleep, I've been watching the tapes I've done of Ola. It's something, to get it all together. The first time I taped my grandmama was under the Joshua tree she's sitting under now.

David says he knows someone who can edit the tapes and make all of it run smoother, but I don't think I want it that way. I like the jerky movements on the first tapes. I'll probably be the only one, though.

Ola sees me through the screen door and motions for me to come out and sit with her. I shut the camera off and go into the heat.

Ola's eyes are closed. She opens them when I get close to her, then takes her headphones off. "I've been listening to relaxation tapes Martha gave me. You can overcome any physical stress if you relax enough."

"Any stress?"

"Any that comes near you."

"Do you believe it, Ola?"

"Looks like I'm going to have to believe it if I want to feel better. I've been thinking about becoming a vegetarian too. Maybe you could help me with that."

"I don't know much about being one. I just am. Never thought about why I don't eat meat."

"I guess it's enough that you don't. I wanted to become one some time ago, but I just didn't take the time to change the habits I've had all my life. I believe that's all it was."

"What about not wanting to eat another living thing, knowing that the animal suffered? What about the suffering? Nothing should suffer."

"You're right. Nothing should suffer. There's enough pain in this world without us inflicting more on each other."

I wanted her to tell me why people suffer, then. I wanted to know why anyone has to go through pain. It didn't look like she was in pain now, but in ten minutes all that could change. It was like she was being held prisoner.

"Do you think you did anything wrong, Ola? I mean—do you think you did something wrong in your life that made this happen, 'cause I don't understand. . . ."

"Emmie, baby. I have cancer. It's not retribution or a curse put on me by some spirit I can't see. It's like any other illness. There is no morality involved. Any disease that kills people and makes them and the people who love them suffer is just that, a horrible disease. Nothing else."

Ola leans back against the tree and closes her eyes again. I sit beside her for a minute and do the same, but the phone starts ringing again in the kitchen. I see Mama and Martha are in the front yard now, so I run to answer the phone.

David's voice relaxes me, and in a minute I'm laughing and promising I'll get together with him before nighttime.

꒱ ꒱ ꒱ **CHAPTER 17**

Ola remembers:

The moment my granddaughter was born, I must have been planting the rosebush that I would name for her. My mama used to name her rosebushes after new babies. My daughter called me half an hour after the baby was born and said that they had named her Emily, and did I think the name was okay.

I cried half the night and didn't know why.

I sent her a hat and little yellow baby bootees that had pom-poms dangling from them. I guess I thought that was the kind of gift a grandmother was supposed to give her grandchild. I almost sealed the box twice before putting in a stone that Martha had brought me back from Africa. She said someone told her it was for luck. Anyway, it sparkled in the sunlight, and I liked to think of it in my small grandbaby's window.

Emmie was two years old when I finally met her. I cried the same as I had the night she was born, and

I think that I scared her. She looked at me with her mouth wide open, and I remember my scarf hitting her in the face.

After that, though, she followed me everywhere and always seemed to be underfoot. I loved her being here. She visited every summer from then on. Some summers, it was just her, but mostly it was her and her mother. Emmie's dad might fly out for a week or two. Emmie and her mom usually stayed two months.

I used to check on them in the middle of the night, just to make sure they were really here.

As she got older, Emmie looked more and more like her mother, and sometimes I called her Diane.

I would look at her sometimes and just want to hug her and keep her by me. She used to cry when she had to leave. Now I cry.

I notice that you can't tell when she's coming down the hall. It's not that she sneaks into a room; she glides like her mother does.

I wonder how long she was at the screen with the camera.

She's sad right now. I know she stays up most nights and worries. I'm glad that I'll get to know her. I thought that I did, but I really don't, it seems.

Even though she's sad, she's got more courage than she can use. I want to stay close to her because I think mine is leaving me. Like eyesight and hearing eventually do.

I saw her climb into the Buick last week. At three in the morning she's going into the dark and driving a car through the desert night. It looked too magical for me to call her back—which was what I should have done, I guess. She was gone by the time I thought about it clearly. I wanted to blame the medication for my lack of judgment, but I let her go the next night too.

I sat and looked at her baby pictures while she was driving through the night and thought about how young fourteen is and how old, these days, it can be.

✾✾✾ CHAPTER 18

I will dream of the desert forever; it will never leave me. Ola says that it doesn't have to. She says the house in Little Rock is mine to come to whenever I want. That won't be for years, though, because she's never coming back to it. I know I can't come back to it while she's alive.

I spend most of the morning touching the walls and sitting on both porches and leaning against every tree. Twice Mama tells me that there's a lot to do before we go to the picnic. She checks off lists and slams cabinets. It's good she has the lists 'cause I think she'd just stand in the middle of the room without them.

I'm standing on the side of the road, watching cars blow by: a few people I know, and a few people I've seen and never met.

Roland and Jake pull into the driveway a little before it's time for the picnic. Jake jumps out of the car and runs over to me, wagging his whole body.

"He's excited about today."

"You think he really knows there's going to be a picnic?"

Roland gets a rubber bone off the front seat and throws it to the side yard. Jake wags after it. "Oh, yeah, he knows. I've been talking about it all morning. He knows *picnic* like he knows *out* and *dinner*." Roland goes into the house.

Jake and I play for a time; then everybody comes out and starts loading Roland's car.

I sit by the Joshua tree. Jake comes over, like he's ready for a nap, and lies down by me. I think he's forgotten about the picnic.

Ola and Roland climb into the car, and Mama looks at me.

"David's picking me up," I say.

"Okay, but you two use some sense on that bike."

Roland calls Jake, but the dog doesn't move from my side. He opens one eye and whines. Roland calls him a traitor. Ola says he'll be okay in the house. I promise to put him there when I leave, and they drive away.

Jake opens both eyes and rolls on his back. I know if he could talk he'd call me a liar. I figure if he knows about the picnic, he knows that I'm lying about David picking me up. I scratch his stomach and throw his bone a couple of feet away; he ignores it and follows me into the house.

I rummage through a box in the hall for a hammer. The house echoes as I wander from room to room, looking for the things that I'll need for the ceremony. Jake follows, his nails clicking down the hall. He pops in and out of rooms and noses around boxes. I find the scarf and hat that I'm looking for in Ola's room. My granddaddy's picture crackles in my back pocket. I put it in my jeans last night after I came back from David's. I grab the keys to the Buick off the hook and leave Jake in the living room.

I shut the door and run to the car but look back at the house and see Jake's big face in the window. He's happier when he's sitting beside me a few minutes later, driving down the road, in the opposite direction from the picnic.

Before I get to the crossroads, I think about sitting in jail and how I'm going to explain having taken the car. It's the first time I've driven it in the daylight. Jake hangs his head out the side so far I think about putting a seat belt around him.

I've been thinking about doing this since I found all of Carl's letters to my granddaddy. The letters got me thinking about remembering people, about living and dying and how people should die the way they lived.

I knew it was something I had to do after I talked to the people at the Highway Store the other day and David last night. . . .

We sat out under the garage light by David's house and watched all the cars passing. I aimed the camera at them, off and on. People would always blow their horns and wave. David caught fireflies and let them go into the night. After he'd freed the last one, he started talking about the powwow.

"It was something, Emmie. It changed me, the powwow, I mean. It's hard to explain. It's your people around you—not like . . . well, you know. It's not like the people who raised me. They're important and I love them, but it's the ceremony. I found ceremony and ritual in Arizona. I never really thought about it all before."

David looked into the light, his head tilted back. I didn't know what to say. I blinked into the light too.

"Do you think about your people, Emmie, your people and their rituals?"

"Not much," I said. "I mean, we get a Christmas tree at Christmas and have Thanksgiving dinner. It's usually seafood, but it's still Thanksgiving. We even have fights with each other during the holidays like everybody else. Is that ritual?"

"Yeah, I guess those are sort of rituals. But I mean the rituals born of who came before you and how they celebrated life and death. It's about our ancestors and how we remember them in this life. They are the reason we are who we are."

Granddaddy's face shone before me while lizards ran just out of the arc of light. I heard only them and David's breathing.

"I've found letters written to my granddaddy, David. He's so real to me now. It's like this is the first time he ever seemed real to me."

David leaned closer, his one blue eye twinkling in the light. "Maybe his spirit walks here."

"Do you believe that?"

"Now I believe it could happen. A year ago I wouldn't have."

I told David about Minnie Jacobs, who told me about ringing the dead to heaven. He sat saying nothing, catching more fireflies, then letting them go. I started thinking about restless souls and ancestors.

It all brought me to this. I turn the radio on and sing along with everything, even if I don't know the words.

The afternoon sun beats down on my head 'til I pull over to the side of the road and get out of the car. I open the trunk and take out the straw hat and scarf I'd put there. I lean against the car and tie the hat down to my head with the scarf. Jake wags when I get in and we take off again.

The desert is motionless in the heat of the day. I watch the heat waves in front of the car and look for the water tower.

I haven't been on this side of town this summer. It's a straight shot from Ola's. I just have to know when to turn off, and I do.

I speed down the road to the shed Martha and David sat on while they watched me drive two summers ago. I park the car by the side of it, and Jake jumps out and chases a lizard into the brush. I get what I need out of the glove compartment, then start to hike to the desert when I see a car turning down the road coming toward me.

Mama parks Roland's car behind the Buick. She sits for a time and watches Jake bouncing around in the desert. For a second I think she's gone to sleep, but the car door opens and soon she's standing by me, looking at the things in my hands.

ঙঙঙ **CHAPTER 19**

Mama's arms are long. They flow when she moves. The wind seems to take them. She sits down on the hard ground and looks off into the desert again. Her face relaxes as she watches Jake chase imaginary birds. He floats in the wind, his furry body looking like a fluff of dust in a breeze. I sit down in the dust beside Mama.

I'd asked Mama, a few days ago, if they ever used sweeps in California. She didn't know for sure, but figured that they did. She didn't think there'd be any sweeps in the desert, though. No water, no farms, no sweeps. She asked me what I knew about sweeps. I told her I'd read about them somewhere. She said "somewhere" as if in a dream, then said that someone had just walked over her grave.

When I told David about it last night, he said that she must have had some kind of vision. Maybe he was right and she saw today.

Mama leans closer, facing me now. I look into her eyes, and they are mine. I think of the ancestors and feel for my mother for the first time. Really the first time. I understand her loss. I feel what it must have been like finding your father dead near a field of kudzu, hot and steamy. I feel for her 'cause she carries the pain and won't forgive her mother for ripping her away from it.

Mama holds my hands. "You have a friend in David. He'll talk when he thinks it's important. He sat at the picnic gazing into space. . . ."

"You knew something was up?"

"Not really. I just felt something might be up, you not there and all."

Mama looks away. "You asked me about sweeps the other day, and I remembered my own grandfather. He toned a sweep when my grandmother died. I must have been three. It was one of my first memories. I loved them all. My parents, grandparents. I even remember loving my grandmother who died when I was so young. I loved Alabama. This place was never home to me."

She looks around her, like she was dropped by a plane a minute ago, seeing it all for the first time. Mama smiles, then reaches down and touches the hammer.

"I never said good-bye to my father, Emmie. This new place happened too fast. Ola thought she was saving me from ugliness. Death really. She did her best, and I guess I've never forgiven her for it."

She pulls me up by my hand and marches me up to what used to be the water tower. "You look like your grandmother in that hat and scarf."

I touch the hat and smile.

"It's time to tone my daddy to Heaven. A few decades late, baby, but . . ."

I stand next to Mama and the twists of metal on the baked ground. I pull out Granddaddy's picture from my pocket, creased now at the corners. I lay it down by the metal. The water tower was as important in the desert as the sweep used to be in Alabama. Granddaddy would understand.

I hold the hammer with Mama, standing on tiptoe for a second to match her height. The hammer shines in the bright sun; then we strike metal. Again and again, until the sound seems natural, a part of the wind. The wind stops and it's just Mama and I, toning the sweep.

When the last tone has been rung, the wind starts blowing again, then settles the dust on the desert. Jake is lying by the car, waiting to jump in. Mama puts her arm around me and slowly walks me to the car.

"Time to celebrate now, baby."

"Yeah," I say, "time to celebrate."

"I'll follow you and Jake back to the house, so you can park Ola's car."

Mama backs away and watches me for a second while I put the hammer in the glove compartment and Granddaddy's picture in my pocket. Jake bounces from one side of the car to the other. Mama jumps into Roland's car and blows me a kiss. She follows me all the way to Ola's, Jake still hanging out the side.

Balloons and streamers, tin cans, and sagebrush decorate the Joshua trees in the park. Mama, Jake, and I step out of the car into a party that looks as if it's come from Mardi Gras. I wander around with the video camera, getting it all on tape. Some people are dressed in costumes, others in street clothes. The air is spicy with Mexican food and barbecue. Jake gets excited, sees Roland and barks, then runs into the crowd.

Mama goes over to a table for punch, and I try to find Ola. I'm hugged at every turn. These people love Ola. The rest spills onto me.

I see Ola now, dancing with Roland. They're dancing a fandango, each holding the end of a handkerchief. It's magic. As the music speeds up, they move as one. Ola's dreads swing from one side to the other.

Margaret Title stands behind me while I tape it all and whispers, "It's a celebration dance. A dance of life." She leaves to talk to a group of people at the food table, thinks twice, then pulls me with her to meet someone.

I meet everybody. I talk and laugh with them all, into the evening shadows. One of the boys in a straw cowboy hat says that I need to learn to fandango. He teaches me, and I dance into the night. I hear Ola laughing every now and then. I see her and Martha on a conga line. All the aunts take part.

When I'm tired, I sit in a company of people who tell me stories about my grandmother, while she dances.

For a few hours after the sun has set, everyone eats and dances by Christmas lights strung everywhere, until they are too tired to do anything but wave good-bye to us.

             Ola sits in the living room, flowers from the picnic all around. Martha says she'll take them home with her. I sit next to Mama, talking to Roland, David, and Martha. I'm safe and comfortable here.

When Roland gets up to leave, well after midnight, so do Martha and David. Martha takes off with him, on the back of his bike, waving to us as she goes. Roland hugs us all, then calls Jake, who sleepily hops in the car and barks until it pulls away. Ola, Mama, and I stand in the night, then walk quietly to the house. We find blankets and fall onto the living room floor, together. I listen to them both breathe. I say my good-byes to the house. It's our last night here.

✌✌✌ CHAPTER 20

I got up early this morning, after almost no sleep at all. I listened to house sounds and stared at shadows that the storage boxes cast, thinking how I'll miss the place.

Martha and David are over early to help with the last of the packing. David says he'll write me at least once a week when I get back to Ohio. He twists his hair and blinks up at the sun, then smiles.

Martha loads up the rest of the things we put out to give to a shelter. She says she'll be going to L.A. again in a few days. I think about all the homeless kids that Martha has taken in and sheltered.

Mama walks through the empty rooms and touches the walls and looks into closets. She's been doing it for the past hour and she never finds anything. She's missed nothing, but she keeps wandering through rooms. Ola watches her and smiles.

The moving van comes for everything that's going to Ohio. We'll be leaving tomorrow on the plane—Martha's driving us to the airport in the Buick. We'll stay at her house tonight.

When she goes tomorrow, Ola will leave three Joshua trees in her front yard and one in the back, a greenhouse full of kudzu that would cover the world if it could, and a 1964 Buick convertible that will now fly through the desert without her.

The desert hasn't really woke up yet. My feet still feel cool in the dust. I have a funny feeling in my stomach.

Mama used to say, "Don't look back. It'll make you an easier person, able to live in this world." Uh-huh.

By the time the moving van hauls onto the highway, the sun has broken on through.